THIS BOOK BELONGS TO

£5.50
UK only

D1143165

CONTENTS

Written and illustrated by Rob Lee with contributions from Stephen Farrell, Anna Llewellyn, Carol and County Studios.

Fireman Sam's jigsaw

Fireman Sam had invented an alarm clock but the trouble was it didn't work very well! "Great fires of London!" puffed Sam as he dashed to work. "I'm late again!" Sam was in such a hurry to get dressed he got all his clothes mixed up! Paste this page on to card and cut out the pieces, following the black lines. Then see if you can complete the picture again.

A ROBOT RUNS RIOT

It was the beginning of the school holidays and Norman Price was looking forward to getting up to lots of mischief as usual. "Brill!" he chuckled.

Norman's mum had other ideas! "You can keep yourself busy doing chores for me this school holiday, my boy," warned Dilys. "Aw Mam!" groaned Norman.

"You can start by sweeping the shop," said Dilys. "Yes Mam," replied Norman. But as soon as his mum was gone he crept out of the window.

Meanwhile, Sam was in his inventing shed. He was trying to invent a robot to help him decorate his house. "This should do nicely," he said.

Soon, Sam was testing his robot. It painted so well; Sam was delighted. "A proper little Picasso, you are," chuckled Sam. "You'll be finished in no time."

Sam pressed some buttons on the robot which programmed it to paint the whole house. Feeling pleased with himself, Sam decided to take a nap.

A little later, while Sam was fast asleep, Norman came snooping around. "Cor! That's brill!" he exclaimed when he spotted Sam's robot.

Norman couldn't resist having a closer look. He crept inside and began poking the robot's buttons. Next thing, the robot whirred out of the house.

Norman raced after the robot. The commotion woke Sam, who got dressed and dashed downstairs. "Oh no!" he cried when he saw the trail of paint.

Sam guessed that Norman Price had been meddling with his robot. "That boy's a menace!" said Sam angrily as he followed the trail of paint.

The robot had soon covered half of Pontypandy in paint. Even Jupiter had been splattered. "Your robot's made quite a mess, Sam!" shouted Steele angrily.

Sam helped Elvis clean up Jupiter, then he went back to tracking down Picasso. The trail of paint seemed to end at Dilys's shop. "Aha!" muttered Sam.

Sam heard loud cries coming from the shop. He looked in and saw the robot running amok, splattering paint all over young Norman!

By the time Sam had switched off the robot Norman was covered. His mum said angrily, "I warned you about getting into mischief. You're grounded!"

"Don't be too hasty, Dilys," said Sam. "Instead of the robot painting my house, Norman can do it. That will keep him busy during the holidays!"

Sam wrote a list of things to be painted. As Norman painted away, Sam laughed. "Any sneaking off, Norman, and I'll set Picasso on you!" Norman groaned.

PAINT POT PUZZLE

NAUGHTY NORMAN HAS JUMBLED UP THE LETTERS ON SAM'S PAINT POTS. CAN YOU HELP HIM RE-ARRANGE THE LETTERS INTO COLOURS, THEN MATCH THE LABELS TO THE CORRECT POTS?

FIT THE FACES!

TRY TO COPY THE FACES OF STATION OFFICER STEELE AND ELVIS CRIDLINGTON INTO THE GRID BELOW.

A PUZZLE ABOUT PONTYPANDY!

HOW WELL DO YOU KNOW THE PEOPLE OF PONTYPANDY?

ACROSS
1. NAME FIREMAN SAM'S ENGINE
5. IF STEELE IS SHORT WHAT IS ELVIS?
6. WHAT IS BELLA'S CAT CALLED?
7. WHAT KIND OF BUSINESS DOES DILYS RUN?
8. WHAT IS THE NAME OF THE STATION OFFICER AT THE STATION?

DOWN
2. WHAT IS SAM'S FAVOURITE VEGETABLE?
3. WHAT IS THE NAME OF THE CAFE IN PONTYPANDY?
4. PENNY IS THE ONLY FEMALE FIREFIGHTER IN PONTYPANDY. WHAT IS HER SURNAME?

FILM FUN!

DILYS IS NOT VERY GOOD AT USING HER VIDEO CAMERA. CAN YOU TELL WHO SHE'S BEEN TRYING TO FILM?

13

COMPUTER CHAOS

Fireman Sam arrived for work at the station. He reported for duty in Station Officer Steele's office.

Steele was emptying his filing cabinet. There were piles of folders on his desk.

"Morning, sir," said Sam.

"Oh you're just in time, Sam," replied Steele. "You can get rid of these old files for me."

"But they're full of important documents and records, sir," said Sam, fingering the files. "Shouldn't you keep them?"

"Don't worry, Sam," said Steele. "Everything in those files is safely stored in here." Steele proudly patted a brand new computer.

"Very, er, swish, sir," said Sam unenthusiastically.

"We've got to change with the times, Sam," said Steele as he began tapping the computer keys.

Next, Sam walked into the mess. Elvis Cridlington was busy writing notes onto his clipboard.

"...Let me see," Elvis muttered to himself. "That's nine eggs, four bags of flour, two saucepans..."

"What on earth are you up to, Elvis?" asked Sam.

"It's called stock taking, Sam," replied Elvis grumpily. "Station Officer Steele wants a list of everything I've got in the mess so that he can record it in his flippin' computer!"

"Seems a very sensible idea to

me," chuckled Sam as he poured himself a mug of tea.

"In that case, you won't mind counting the hoses, extinguishers and ladders," said Elvis, "because Station Officer Steele wants a list of those next!"

Sam groaned.

Later that day, Sam and Elvis took their lists to Steele's office.

"Good work, men," said Steele. "After lunch we'll practise call out drills. We'll imagine there's a fire at Pandy Station on the other side of Newtown."

"I'd better study the map, sir," said Sam. "We haven't had a call out there for years."

"No need Sam," replied Steele, triumphantly patting his computer. "Maps of the whole of Wales are stored in here!"

Steele demonstrated by pressing a key on the computer and a map of Newtown appeared on the screen. Sam and Elvis were impressed.

Later, Steele pressed the alarm bells and dashed into the mess. "Call out, men!" he shouted. "Fire at Pandy Station. Jump to it!"

Sam and Elvis raced into action. Before long they were speeding towards Newtown, sirens blaring.

Sam lifted the phone in Jupiter's cab and asked for instructions. In his office, Steele studied the computer's map and barked orders down the phone. "Head down Newtown Road, Sam, and take the second right past the hospital, then first left at the gas works..."

Sam followed Steele's directions

as he steered Jupiter through the countryside. Sam looked puzzled.

"That's odd," he muttered into the phone. "I've followed your directions, sir, but I didn't see a hospital or the gas works..."

"Nonsense. The computer can't be wrong," interrupted Steele. "You should have a straight road to Newtown now. Full speed and you'll be there in two minutes!"

Sam pressed the accelerator pedal and they were soon racing along the road at top speed. Suddenly Sam and Elvis noticed they were heading straight for a pond.

"Oh no!" cried Elvis as Jupiter flew off the road and landed in a large pond with a mighty splash!

"Great Fires of London!" exclaimed Sam as he looked out of the window to see that they were stranded in the middle of the pond.

Just then Steele's voice came over the telephone.

"Have you reached Pandy Station yet, Sam?" asked Steele.

"Not unless it's a submarine station, sir!" replied Sam grimly. "We're in about three feet of water!"

Luckily, Jupiter managed to reverse out of the pond. Sam steered the dripping fire engine back to the station. When they arrived, Steele was in his office angrily tapping the computer's keys.

"No wonder I sent you in the wrong direction, Sam," said Steele crossly.
"The map on the screen is upside down. There must be a gremlin in the works!"

"Perhaps a certain Station Officer

doesn't know how to use it," muttered Sam under his breath. Steele angrily began twiddling away at the computer with his screwdriver.

"I wouldn't do that, sir," said Sam anxiously. "That's a job for experts."

"Nonsense!" replied Steele, just before the computer blew up with a loud BANG!

"Good gracious!" cried Steele.

Sam grabbed a fire extinguisher and quickly sprayed foam over the smouldering computer.

"I think your computer's had it, sir," said Elvis as he examined the soggy remains. Steele groaned.

Later in the mess, Steele glumly sipped tea with Elvis.

"It's a disaster," wailed Steele. "All

the station's records went up in smoke with the computer!"

Just then, Sam walked in carrying the folders that Steele had asked him to throw out.

"Just as well I didn't throw these out then, sir!" laughed Sam. "I had a funny feeling you wouldn't get on with that new-fangled computer!"

"Well done, Sam!" exclaimed a very relieved Steele.

"That will teach an old dog like me not to try to learn new tricks!"

"I dunno, sir," piped up Elvis. "There's nothing wrong in changing with the times."

Just then a pot of Elvis's stew bubbled out all over the stove. "It seems some things never change, Elvis!" chuckled Sam.

FLYING COLOURS!

FIREMAN SAM WAS TESTING HIS NEW INVENTION. UNFORTUNATELY IT WENT HAYWIRE AND DRAINED MOST OF THE COLOUR FROM THE PICTURE. CAN YOU COLOUR IT BACK IN?

CRUMBS!

SAM HAS ACCIDENTALLY KNOCKED OVER ELVIS'S TRAY OF CAKES. HOW MANY ARE THERE AND WHICH TWO ARE IDENTICAL?

AMAZING MAZE!

HELP SAM FIND HIS WAY THROUGH THE MAZE TO JUPITER!

CANDY FLOSS CAPERS

It was quiet at Pontypandy Fire Station. Fireman Sam popped into Station Officer Steele's office to see if there was any work that needed doing.

Steele was busy reading his newspaper. "It says here, Sam," said Steele, "that Newtown are having a raffle to raise funds for charity. That sounds interesting."

"As we're quiet, perhaps we could raise some money for charity," suggested Sam. "How about a fête?" "Grand idea!" replied Steele. "Let's get started right away."

Soon, Sam and the crew were busy organising the fête. Everyone in Pontypandy helped. Bella made some of her special Italian cakes to sell.

The twins, Sarah and James, gave Sam a box of toys. "They can be used as prizes," said Sarah. "Very generous of you," replied Sam.

Norman Price offered to donate his skateboard. "It would be a great prize, Norman," said Sam. "But a wheel is missing!" Norman scratched his chin.

Norman's mum Dilys gave Sam a box of coconuts. "You could use these for a coconut shy," she suggested. "Smashing idea Dilys!" replied Sam.

Meanwhile, Norman had made his way to Pontypandy scrapyard. "Perhaps I can find a spare wheel for my skateboard here," he wondered.

"There's one!" he exclaimed. Suddenly, a heavy pipe he was leaning on gave way and Norman slipped. "Help!" he cried as he tumbled down.

"Help! I'm stuck!" cried Norman. Luckily, Sarah and James were passing by. "Don't worry, Norman," called James. "We'll phone the fire station."

Sam was soon on the scene. "I'll have you out of here in two shakes, Norman," said Sam as he got to work with his special metal cutters.

"Thanks, Sam!" said Norman as Sam freed him. Just then, Sam saw something interesting. "That old washing machine could come in handy."

Soon the fête was ready. Everybody had lots of fun at the different stalls and sideshows. Bella loved the hoop-la. "Ees bellisima!" she cried.

"The lucky dip is brill!" said Norman to Trevor. "You win every time." Trevor just hoped Norman hadn't left a mouse trap in the dip, like he did last time.

Sam had fixed the old washing machine he'd found at the scrapyard and turned it into a candy floss machine! His stand soon made lots of money for the charity. "Great idea, Sam," said Steele. "Thank you, sir," chuckled Sam. "You could say my candy floss is selling like hot cakes!" Sam and Steele chuckled.

SPOT THE DIFFERENCE

SAM AND CREW ARE IN THE STATION MESS.
THE TWO PICTURES ARE NOT QUITE THE
SAME. HAVE A CLOSE LOOK AT BOTH PICTURES — THERE
ARE EIGHT DIFFERENCES IN THE BOTTOM PICTURE,
CAN YOU SPOT THEM?

DOT - TO - DOT

SARAH HAS FOUND ONE OF HER OLD TOYS. JOIN THE DOTS AND DISCOVER WHAT IT IS.

A PICTURE TO COLOUR

HOPPING MAD!

NORMAN'S FROG HAS ESCAPED AND FRIGHTENED HIS MUM DILYS. THERE ARE FOUR MORE HIDING IN THE SHOP. CAN YOU FIND THEM? WHEN YOU HAVE DONE THIS YOU CAN COLOUR THE PAGE.

Sam and the crew are trying to rescue Norman from a flooded river. Help them by placing different coloured counters on the **START** and take it in turns to throw a dice. Follow any instructions that you land on. If you land on a **BLUE SQUARE** you must miss a go. The first player to reach **FINISH** is the winner!

DICE GAME

START

1

STOP TO
RESCUE DILYS.
MISS A
TURN.

2

3

4

5

6 PONTY
FLOODE
RESCUE
GO BAC

FISHY TALES

Sam decided to call into Bella's cafe for his favourite cheese and chutney sandwiches.

"Morning, Sam," sighed Bella who was serving the twins, Sarah and James.

"What's up, Bella?" asked Sam. "You seem to be out of sorts." "No wonder," she replied. "I'm-a so busy! I've got to collect a parcel from the station and then I've-a got to peel all these potatoes…"

"Calm down, Bella," interrupted Sam. "When I've finished my shift I'll come down and give you a hand."

Sarah piped up, "And James and I could collect your parcel from the station for you."

"Ah bellissima!" smiled Bella. "You're so kind."

Sam left the cafe and headed for the station.

Inside the mess room Elvis was cooking breakfast for Station Officer Steele when Sam arrived.

"You're just in time for breakfast," said Elvis, brandishing his frying pan under Sam's nose. Sam groaned as he examined the burnt offerings. "Er, I'll stick to my sandwiches if

32

you don't mind, Elvis," sighed Sam.

"As soon as you've finished breakfast I want you to pop over to Newtown Station to collect some supplies, Sam," said Steele.

"Right-o sir," replied Sam. Meanwhile, Sarah and James

had picked up Bella's parcel at Pontypandy Station. They walked back to town along the riverbank.

"It's marked fragile," said James, pointing at the parcel's label. "I wonder what's inside?"

"I don't know," replied Sarah. "But be careful it doesn't get damaged."

Sarah spotted something in the river and shouted excitedly, "Look James! There's an eel!"

"Brill!" cried James, leaning over the bridge. "I wonder if it's an electric eel?" Unfortunately in his excitement, James dropped the parcel into the river. "Oh no!" he cried as the

parcel was swept downstream.

"Hurry, James!" shouted Sarah as she sprinted down the riverbank. "Perhaps we can catch up with it."
Meanwhile downstream, Trevor Evans was doing a spot of fishing. He wasn't enjoying much success, however. "Daro!" he groaned as he landed a rusty old kettle! "It's more like a scrapyard than a river!" He put the kettle with all the other bits of junk he had caught.

"The nearest I've caught to a fish is an old sardine can."
Suddenly Bella's parcel floated into view.
"What on earth...?" exclaimed Trevor as he netted the parcel. He read the label. "It's addressed to Bella," he muttered, scratching his head. "I've heard of air mail but not river mail!"
Just then Sarah and James raced along the bank towards him.
"Slow down, my little sugar

lumps," chuckled Trevor as the twins arrived puffing and panting. "Easy does it. Where's the fire?"

"Thank goodness!" puffed James as he spotted the package in Trevor's hands.

"Well done, Trevor," said Sarah.
"Bella would have been upset if we'd lost her parcel."

"Something tells me she's not going to be too pleased anyway," warned Trevor as he examined the soggy package. "Whatever's inside will be ruined!"

Sarah and James gulped nervously.

"Trevor's right," groaned Sarah.

Meanwhile, Sam was on his way back from Newtown. As he drove Jupiter along the riverbank he spotted Trevor and the twins. He pulled over and climbed down. When he arrived on the scene the twins explained what had happened.

"I'll give you both a lift to Bella's," said Sam, before adding hopefully. "Let's hope no harm's done."

"I'll come with you," said
Trevor. "I'm not having much
luck fishing. First I'd better find
a safe place for all this junk I've
caught."

Sam eyed the bits of scrap
and metal and scratched his
chin thoughtfully. "Load them
onto Jupiter, Trev," he chuckled.
"They might come in very useful
if Bella needs cheering up!"

Later, Bella was busy peeling
potatoes when Sam and the
twins arrived.

"Ah, bellisima, you've got my
parcel," smiled Bella.

"Er, I'm sorry, B-Bella,"
stuttered James nervously,
handing over the dripping
parcel. "I dropped it in the river.

I hope it's not ruined."

Bella, to everyone's
amazement, burst out laughing.
She opened the parcel to reveal
a pair of large, plump fish.

"Ruined? They-a came from a
river in the first place!"

Sam and the twins laughed
with relief.

"All that worrying for nothing,"
chuckled James.

"As you've been so kind you
can all-a come round for tea
later!" beamed Bella.

"Brill!" cried the twins.

A little later Sam was busy in
his shed. "These bits of junk
have come in very handy," he
muttered as he busily screwed
pieces of metal together.

"If I just attach this thingamyjig to the sprocket catch like so...that's it, perfect!"

That evening the twins licked their lips as Bella prepared fish and chips for them.

"Ees nearly ready," said Bella. "I hope Sam's not late."

Just then Sam arrived carrying a strange contraption. "What's that, Uncle Sam?" asked Sarah and James curiously.

"It's a little present I've invented for Bella," replied Sam as he placed it on the counter.

"What does it do?" asked Bella.

"Simple!" explained Sam as he put a potato into the funnel of the machine. Seconds later, out popped a small pile of chipped potatoes. "It's a Fireman Sam patented potato peeler and chipper!"

Brill!" cried the twins.

"Ees fantastic, Sam!" exclaimed Bella.

As Sam and the twins tucked into their fish and chips, Bella happily popped potatoes into the machine one after another.

"It looks like Bella's suddenly taken quite a shine to peeling potatoes!" chuckled Sam.

The twins giggled.

SILHOUETTES

THERE ARE 3 SILHOUETTES OF SAM'S INVENTION ON THIS PAGE.
WHICH ONE IS ACCURATE?

A

B

C

TO THE RESCUE!

THE FOUR PICTURES BELOW CONTAIN DETAILS OF THE
BIG PICTURE. CAN YOU TELL WHICH PART OF THE BIG
PICTURE THEY COME FROM? EACH PICTURE HAS
SOMETHING MISSING. CAN YOU SPOT IT?

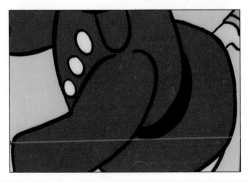

THREE'S A CROWD

IN THE BOX BELOW YOU WILL FIND SEVERAL
ITEMS THAT APPEAR IN THE PICTURE
ABOVE. THREE ITEMS HOWEVER DO NOT.
CAN YOU SPOT WHICH ONES THEY ARE?

JUMBLED UP!

IN THIS STORY SAM GETS CALLED OUT TO A FIRE. THE PICTURES HAVE GOT ALL JUMBLED UP. CAN YOU TELL WHAT ORDER THEY SHOULD BE IN? TO GIVE YOU A CLUE, THE FIRST PICTURE IS THE ONE WITH THE ALARM BELLS!

THE BIG GAME

Sam was excited. Today was the day of the big football game between City and United. Then he remembered he was working today.

"Daro!" he groaned as he trudged into the station. "Fancy missing the game!" "Perhaps Steele will let us watch it on telly," said Elvis, hopefully.

But Steele had plans for a spring-clean of the station. He had a whole list of jobs for the crew. Elvis and Sam groaned. "Jump to it, men!" barked Steele.

Station Officer Steele ordered Sam and Elvis to wash Jupiter, tidy up the station and give the garage doors a fresh coat of brand new paint.

Later, Norman appeared. "Aren't you going to watch the big game on TV?" he asked. "Not while Steele's keeping an eye on us!" muttered Sam.

Norman wandered into the station. He spotted Steele taking a nap. "Cor!" he chuckled. "I've got an idea of how I can help Elvis and Sam."

He took a crayon from his pocket and dabbed spots on Steele's face. "When he wakes up he'll think he's ill and go home," giggled Norman.

But by the time Sam and Elvis appeared, Steele was wiping the spots off his face. "Somebody's been playing tricks on me!" said Steele angrily.

Station Officer Steele was so angry he gave Sam and Elvis even more work to do. "We'll never get to see the game now!" moaned Elvis, grumpily.

Later, Steele looked out of his office window to keep an eye on Sam and Elvis when he spotted a skateboard that Norman had left lying around.

"That's a dangerous place to leave a skateboard," said Steele. He was about to move it when he had a thought. "I wonder..." he muttered.

"I've never tried a skateboard before," said Steele, itching to have a go. Next thing he was on the skateboard whizzing around the fire station.

"Fantastic!" cried Steele as he raced along. "Time to try a wheelie," he laughed. But he suddenly hit the kerb and went flying. "WHOAA!" he wailed.

Sam, Elvis and Norman heard the commotion and dashed to Steele who was feeling very groggy. "Are you OK, sir?" asked Sam. "You look quite pale."

Steele decided that he should go home and rest. "Lucky you left your skateboard where you did, Norman," said Elvis later, "otherwise we'd never have

had time to watch the match!" "In fact," said Sam, "as we'll be busy watching the game you can be acting station officer, Norman." Norman beamed.

CROSSWORD PUZZLE

ACROSS

1. IRON, STEEL, ETC.
4. UNWELL
6. PAT, BACKWARDS
7. COLOUR
9. A LENGTH OF.........

DOWN

1. MYSELF
2. JOURNEY
3. SMALL
5. THE EARTH IS ONE
6. RIP
8. NOT DOWN

THAT'S ODD!

SAM, TREVOR AND PENNY HAVE BEEN DRAWN TWICE. IN THE BOTTOM ROW EACH OF THEM HAVE TWO THINGS MISSING. TRY TO SPOT THEM.

THE TWINS ARE IN A TANGLE!

SARAH WANTS TO PLAY A SKIPPING GAME WITH JAMES BUT SHE'S NOT SURE WHICH IS HIS ROPE. CAN YOU HELP HER FIND IT?

1

2

3

PUZZLE POSER!

WHEN SAM FINISHED HIS JIGSAW PUZZLE HE REALISED A PIECE WAS MISSING. HE TRIED TO DRAW A PIECE TO FIT THE PICTURE. IT TOOK HIM THREE GOES TO GET IT RIGHT. WHICH ONE OF THE THREE PIECES BELOW FIT THE PICTURE ACCURATELY?

1 **2** **3**

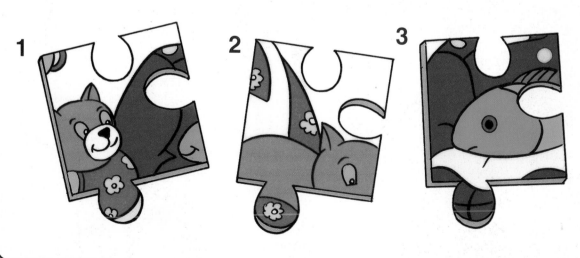

LOST AND FOUND

Sam was driving to the station in Jupiter. Jupiter's engine was coughing and spluttering.

"That doesn't sound too healthy," muttered Sam.

As he drove through the country lanes Sam spotted Norman Price. He noticed that Norman was carrying a little cardboard box. "Hello, Norman," he called. "What have you got there?"

"It's my new pet mouse," replied Norman, opening the box. "He's called Hector. Would you like to stroke him?"

Sam was admiring Hector when the mouse jumped out of Norman's hand and scampered into the long grass.

"Oh no!" cried Norman.

"Quickly!" called Sam. "After him before he gets away!"

Sam and Norman tried to catch the mouse but he had disappeared into the long grass.

After a while Sam said, "It could take hours to find him and I'm due back at the station."

"Don't worry, Sam," said Norman. "I'll find him."

Sam drove off with a wave. "Good luck!" he called.

Soon Sam pulled into the station. He noticed that Jupiter's engine was sounding even worse. Not only was it coughing and spluttering, now it was squeaking as well!

"I think Jupiter could do with a good service," said Sam as he walked into the mess.

"I'll give you a hand when I've finished cooking breakfast," offered Elvis.

"I think breakfast is cooked

already," chuckled Sam, pointing to the toaster where the toast was merrily burning to a crisp.

"Oh no!" groaned Elvis.

Meanwhile, Norman was having no luck finding Hector. Just then Sarah and James appeared. Norman explained what had happened.

"We'll help you find him," said Sarah. "He can't be too far away."

They all headed through the long grass until suddenly Norman felt the ground give way beneath his feet. "Whoaa!" he cried as he fell into a deep, dark hole.

"Are you alright Norman?" shouted Sarah.

"I-I think so," replied Norman. "But I can't climb out. It's too steep."

"Don't worry," called James. "We'll get help!" James remembered there

was a phone box down the lane. He and Sarah ran to it and phoned the fire station.

Station Officer Steele took the call. "We'll be there in two minutes," he replied, before warning Sarah and James. "In the meantime stay well back from the hole!"

At that moment, Sam and Elvis were in the garage fixing Jupiter. They'd replaced lots of parts until the engine sounded as good as new, except for one thing...they could still hear a squeaky noise! Sam and Elvis were baffled. "It beats me," sighed Sam. "I've oiled everything, how can it be squeaking?"

Just then Steele hurried into the garage. "Quickly, men!" he called. "Norman's fallen into a hole near Pandy Lane. Jump to it!" Steele and the crew sprang into action.

they reached the entrance to the mine.

"Be careful, Sam," warned Steele as Sam put on his oxygen mask and entered the mine shaft.

Sam shone his torch into the darkness and made his way deeper into the tunnel, calling Norman's name. Eventually Norman saw the torchlight and shouted, "Over here, Sam!"

"You're safe now, Norman," said Sam as he helped him to his feet and guided him out of the tunnel. Just as they had stepped outside, part of the roof collapsed behind them.

"Phew! That was close!" exclaimed Sam.

"Good work, Sam," beamed Steele.

"There's no harm done," said Sam

They jumped aboard Jupiter and in seconds were roaring through Pontypandy, siren's blaring.

In minutes, Jupiter was speeding across the fields towards Sarah and James. As the crew jumped down Sarah pointed towards the hole.

"Don't worry, Norman," called Steele. "We'll have you out in no time."

"It's an old mine shaft," said Sam, examining the hole. "It would be safer if we used the main entrance."

They climbed down the hill until

as he patted the dust off Norman. "At least nothing a piping hot mug of tea back at the station won't cure!"

"What about Hector?" wondered Norman.

"He's probably miles away, Norman," replied Sam sadly. "I'm afraid you'll never find him now."

They all climbed aboard Jupiter and were soon pulling up at the station.

As Sam climbed down he heard the squeaking again. He scratched his chin thoughtfully. "That's strange. I can hear the squeaking but the engine has stopped!" He followed the sound of the squeaking to one of Jupiter's lockers. He quickly opened the locker and was amazed to see Norman's mouse Hector hidden amongst the hoses and extinguishers. "Great Fires of London!" cried Sam.

"So that's what was causing the squeaking. Hector must have stowed away on board Jupiter when we were searching the fields for him!"

"Brill!" cried Norman excitedly.

Soon they were all enjoying a mug of tea in the mess. Norman made sure that Hector was safely back in his box.

"I'm sorry I caused so much trouble," said Norman.

"It wasn't your fault, Norman," replied Sam. "Besides, Jupiter got the best service of its life. It's running as good as new, thanks to Hector!"

Hector squeaked and everybody laughed.

PICTURE THIS!

HELP FIREMAN SAM DRAW
TREVOR EVANS BY
CAREFULLY COPYING THE
LITTLE SQUARES INTO THE
BIG SQUARES!

FIND THE WORD

NORMAN HAS HIDDEN ONE OF SAM'S TOOLS.
IF YOU TAKE THE INITIAL OF EACH OF THE ITEMS
CIRCLED BELOW AND PUT THEM IN THE RIGHT
ORDER YOU WILL FIND THE NAME OF THE MISSING TOOL.

55

STRANGE HAPPENINGS

FIREMAN SAM IS ENJOYING A TEA PARTY WITH PENNY MORRIS AND THE TWINS, SARAH AND JAMES. IF YOU LOOK CLOSELY YOU WILL FIND SIX THINGS IN THE PICTURE THAT ARE STRANGE. CAN YOU SPOT THEM?

PERFECT PARTNERS

NEARLY ALL THE ITEMS BELOW HAVE A PARTNER ON THE PAGE. CAN YOU MATCH THEM? THREE ITEMS ARE ODD. TRY TO SPOT THEM.

ODD ONES OUT: WELLINGTON. CAP. CUP.

NORMAN PRICE'S PRANKS!

Pontypandy is a nice, peaceful little town until naughty Norman Price decides it's time to be mischievous. Today was one of those days. Norman rubbed his hands with glee.

Norman was in his bedroom going through his toys. He came across his old chemistry set and joke box. "Cor, brill!" he chuckled. "I can have great fun with these!"

Later that day, Sam went into Bella's cafe for a cup of tea. Just then, Norman came scuttling out. "He seems in a bit of a hurry," muttered Sam.

Inside, Bella was moaning because her dishwasher had broken down. "I've-a-got a mountain of dishes to wash," groaned Bella. "I'm-a-so busy!"

Just then a mouse shot along the counter. "EEK!" cried Bella, who was terrified of mice. She dropped her dishes with an almighty SMASH!

"It's only a toy," said Sam. "I bet it was left by Norman. That's why he was in a hurry!" "At-a-least I've got less dishes to wash," sighed Bella.

Meanwhile, Norman's mum, Dilys Price was tidying her shop. She found a strange tin on the counter. She picked it up and examined it curiously.

"I wonder what's in here?" she muttered. As she opened it lots of joke snakes flew into the air. "HELP!" she wailed. "I'm being attacked!"

Up at Pontypandy Fire Station, Elvis had seen Norman hanging around. "What's he up to?" puzzled Elvis until he saw the colour of his mashed potato!

"You menace!" cried Elvis as he raced after Norman. "What's wrong with bright green mashed potato?" chuckled Norman as he ran off.

Norman dashed across the station yard and bumped straight into Fireman Sam. "You seem in a hurry," said Sam. "I wonder what mischief you're up to?"

Elvis arrived and explained to Sam about Norman and his trick food colouring mixture. "I was only playing," stuttered Norman nervously. "Honest."

"As you like playing around in the kitchen, Norman," said Sam, "I know the very place for you." "Where are we going?" asked Norman. "You'll see!" chuckled Sam.

Bella was delighted at Sam's idea that Norman should pay for her broken dishes by washing all the dirty ones. "Bellisima," laughed Bella.

"That should help Bella," laughed Sam as he climbed aboard Jupiter. "And what's more, it should keep everybody safe from Norman's pranks!"

"Oh no!" he cried as he smelled a horrible pong. Sam had sat on a stink bomb that Norman had left in Jupiter. "Norman flippin' Price!" groaned Sam.